"This upbeat series really encourages the very young to 'go for it!' with bright vocabulary, illustration and concept . . . These lovely books are true boosters for preschool confidence, self-concept and beginning reading skills."
—*School Library Journal*

"Where's my daddy?" asks Bear. But nobody can help Bear find him—not the milkman, not the letter carrier, not even Mommy, though she can find a kiss for him. But Bear isn't one to give up easily, and in the end his perseverance pays off—for there's Daddy!

Bear's persistent search is sure to offer encouragement to small children who, like Bear, are just beginning to do things "all by themselves."

Author of many outstanding books for young people, SHIGEO WATANABE has also translated many of the world's great children's books into Japanese. Acclaimed illustrator YASUO OHTOMO brings to this book the warmth, simplicity, and humor for which he is especially known. Both he and Mr. Watanabe live near Tokyo, Japan.

Other books
by Shigeo Watanabe

I Can Do It All By Myself books
How do I put it on?
An American Library Association
Notable Children's Book
What a good lunch!
Get set! Go!
I'm king of the castle!
I can ride it!
Where's my daddy?
I can build a house!
I can take a walk!

I Love To Do Things With Daddy books
Daddy, play with me!

Text copyright © 1979 by Shigeo Watanabe.
Illustrations copyright © 1979 by Yasuo Ohtomo.
American text copyright © 1982 by Philomel Books.
All rights reserved. This book, or parts thereof,
may not be reproduced in any form without permission
in writing from the publisher.
Philomel Books, a division of The Putnam & Grosset Group,
200 Madison Avenue, New York, NY 10016.
Sandcastle Books and the Sandcastle logo are trademarks
belonging to The Putnam & Grosset Group.
First Sandcastle Books edition, 1992.
Printed in Hong Kong.
Library of Congress Cataloging in Publication Data
Watanabe, Shigeo, 1928–   Where's my daddy?
Summary: A little bear asks passersby
if they have seen his daddy.
[1. Fathers—Fiction. 2. Bears—Fiction]
1. Ohtomo, Yasuo, II. Title.
PZ7.W2615Wh 1980 [E] 79-19347
ISBN 0-399-21852-1 (GB)
1 3 5 7 9 10 8 6 4 2
(revised edition)
ISBN 0-399-22427-0 (Sandcastle)
1 3 5 7 9 10 8 6 4 2
First Sandcastle Books Impression

Where's my daddy?

Adapted from a Story by
Shigeo Watanabe
Pictures by Yasuo Ohtomo

PHILOMEL BOOKS

Where's my daddy?
I can find him all by myself.
Maybe he's under
these dandelions.

No!

Oh, hello, birds.
Have you seen my daddy?

No!

No!

Hello, Cat.
Have you seen my daddy?

Sorry!
I have no time to talk!

Hello, Milkman.
Have you seen my daddy?

No!

Hello, Paper Seller.
Have you seen my daddy?

No, but I left his newspaper
at your house.

Hello, Letter Carrier.
Have you seen my daddy?

No! But I have a letter for him.

Hello, Mommy.
Have you seen Daddy?

No,
but I've got a kiss for you.

Thank you, Mommy,
but I'm still looking for Daddy.

Hello, Daddy! There you are!

I found you
all by myself!

Library of Congress Cataloging in Publication Data
Watanabe, Shigeo, 1928–   Where's my daddy?
Summary: A little bear asks passersby
if they have seen his daddy.
[1. Fathers—Fiction. 2. Bears—Fiction]
1. Ohtomo, Yasuo, II. Title.
PZ7.W2615Wh   1980   [E]   79-19347
ISBN 0-399-21852-1 (GB)
ISBN 0-399-21851-3 (pbk)
First GB Edition (revised)
First Paperback Edition (revised)